P9-AGI-670

Ladybird

Billy Goats Gruff

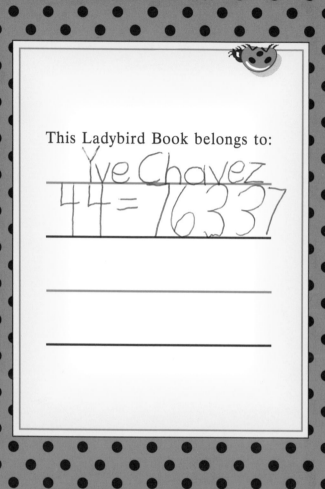

This Ladybird Book belongs to:

Yve Chavez

44 = 76.337

Revised edition

Ladybird Books Inc., Auburn, Maine 04210, U.S.A.
Published by Ladybird Books Ltd., Loughborough, Leicestershire, U.K.

© LADYBIRD BOOKS LTD. 1993
LADYBIRD and the associated pictorial device are trademarks of Ladybird Books Ltd.
All rights reserved. No part of this publication may be reproduced,
stored in a retrieval system, or transmitted in any form or by any
means, electronic, mechanical, photocopying, recording or otherwise,
without the prior consent of the copyright owner.

Printed in Canada.

Billy Goats Gruff

by Fran Hunia

illustrated by John Dyke

This is
little billy goat Gruff.

He likes to jump.

This is
middle-sized
billy goat Gruff.

He likes
to have fun.

This is
big billy goat Gruff.

He likes
to eat grass.

Here is a bridge.

A big troll
lives under
the bridge.

The billy goats Gruff
want to go
over the bridge
for some grass.

Trip, trap, trip, trap,
trip, trap.

Little billy goat Gruff
is on the bridge.

Up jumps the troll.

He says,
"I want
to eat you up."

"No, no," says
little billy goat Gruff.

"Here comes
middle-sized
billy goat Gruff.

He is big and fat.

You can eat **him** up!"

"Yes," says the troll.
"Yes, I can.
You can go over
the bridge."

Trip, trap,
trip, trap, trip, trap.

Little billy goat Gruff
is over the bridge.

24

Middle-sized
billy goat Gruff
looks up.

"Little billy goat Gruff
is over the bridge,"
he says.

"He has some grass
to eat.

I can go
over the bridge
for some grass, too."

Trip, trap,
trip, trap, trip, trap.

Middle-sized
billy goat Gruff
is on the bridge.

Up jumps the troll.

He says, "I want
to eat you up."

"No, no," says middle-sized billy goat Gruff.

"Here comes big billy goat Gruff.

He is big and fat.

You can eat **him** up."

"Yes," says the troll.

"You can go
over the bridge."

Trip, trap, trip, trap,
trip, trap.

Middle-sized
billy goat Gruff
is over the bridge.

Big billy goat Gruff
looks up.

"Little billy goat Gruff
and middle-sized
billy goat Gruff
are over the bridge,"
he says.

"I can go
over the bridge
for some grass, too."

Trip, trap,
trip, trap, trip, trap.

Big billy goat Gruff
is on the bridge.

Up jumps the troll.

He says,
"I want to eat
you up."

"No, no," says
big billy goat Gruff.
"I want to eat
you up."

Up goes the troll.

He goes
SPLASH
into the water.

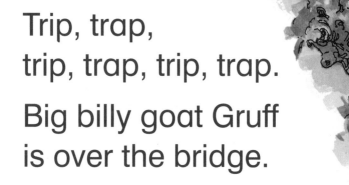

Trip, trap,
trip, trap, trip, trap.

Big billy goat Gruff
is over the bridge.

The billy goats Gruff
have fun in the grass.

They eat and eat
and eat.

"We like it here,"
they say.

Read It Yourself storybooks
are specially designed for beginning readers.
They present the stories children know and
love best, told in simple, easy-to-read language.
The vocabulary of each story is carefully selected
to introduce the most frequently used words
in the English language, and attractive
full-color illustrations help move the story along.
Read It Yourself storybooks
help build skills and boost confidence.

LADYBIRD BOOKS, INC.
Auburn, Maine 04210
Published by LADYBIRD BOOKS LTD.
Loughborough, Leicestershire, U.K.
LADYBIRD and the associated pictorial
device are trademarks of Ladybird Books Ltd.
Printed in Canada.

$ 2.25

ISBN 0-7214-5402-X

0 19987 05402 9